THIS CANDLEWICK BOOK BELONGS TO:

_____

_____

_____

To Ronald, who loves strawberry pie
D. D.

For Doug, Samantha, Carter, and Duffy
A. C.

Text copyright © 2007 by Dayle Ann Dodds
Illustrations copyright © 2007 by Abby Carter

First paperback edition 2009

The Library of Congress has cataloged the hardcover edition as follows:

Dodds, Dayle Ann.
Full House : an invitation to fractions / Dayle Ann Dodds ; illustrated by Abby Carter. — 1st ed.
p.   cm.
ISBN 978-0-7636-2468-2 (hardcover)
1. Fractions — Juvenile literature.   I. Carter, Abby, ill.   II. Title.
QA117.D63 2007
513.2'6 – dc22   2006051847

ISBN 978-0-7636-4130-6 (paperback)

11 12 13 14 15 16 CCP 12 11 10 9 8 7 6 5 4

Printed in Shenzhen, Guangdong, China

This book was typeset in Cafeteria.
The illustrations were done in watercolor and black colored pencil.

Candlewick Press
99 Dover Street
Somerville, Massachusetts 02144

visit us at www.candlewick.com

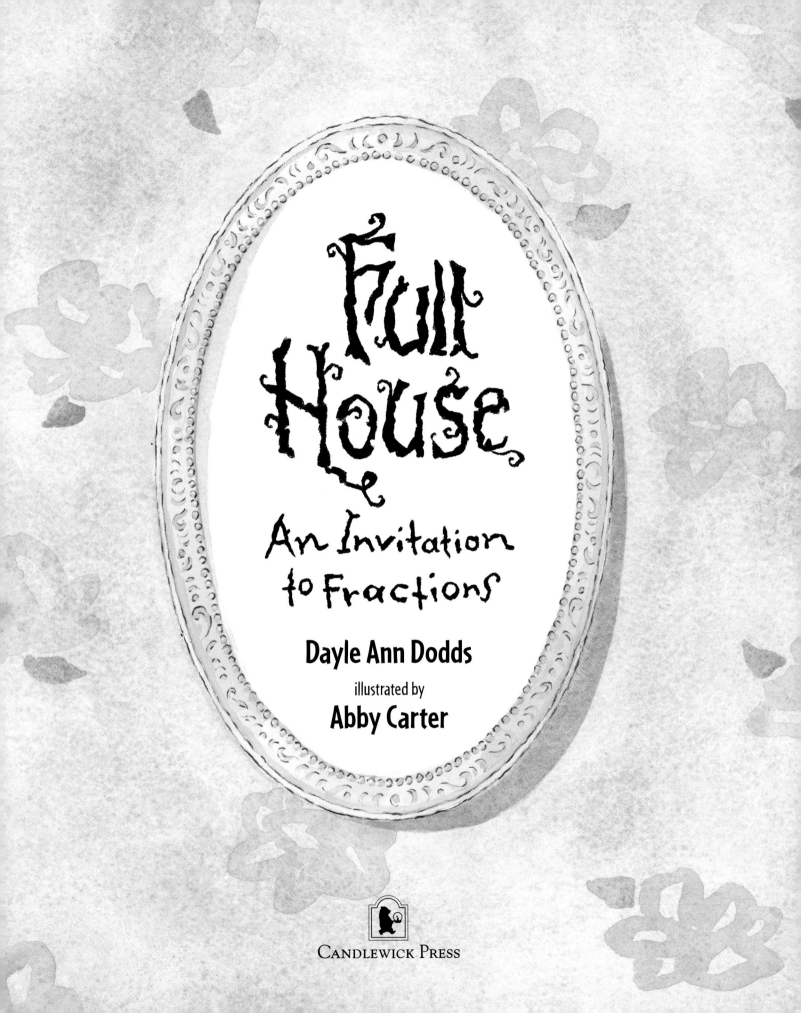

Full House

An Invitation to Fractions

Dayle Ann Dodds

illustrated by
Abby Carter

CANDLEWICK PRESS

The Strawberry Inn was run by Miss Bloom.
Happy was she to fill every room.

With one for herself and five for the guests,
there were six rooms in all for a cozy night's rest.

The
Strawberry Inn

VACANCY

Knock-
knock!

went the door.

Ding-dong!

the bell rang.

"Welcome, welcome," Miss Bloom sang.

"Aye, a rest, that be my wish,"
said Sea Captain Duffy, who smelled just like fish.

So Sea Captain Duffy, all tired and done,
followed Miss Bloom to Room Number 1.

Now ONE room of SIX had a guest for the night.
To fill up the inn would be pure delight.

$\dfrac{1}{6}$

Knock-knock! went the door. *Ding-dong!* the bell rang.
"Welcome, welcome," Miss Bloom sang.

"Charmed, I'm sure," said the Duchess Boofaye.
"Smoochie and I are on holiday."

So the Duchess Boofaye, in sapphires of blue,
followed Miss Bloom to Room Number 2.

Now TWO rooms of SIX had guests for the night.
To fill up the inn would be pure delight!

Knock-knock! went the door. *Ding-dong!* the bell rang.
"Welcome, welcome," Miss Bloom sang.

"Care for a hairbrush, a toothbrush, a comb?
Or maybe a vacuum?" said Salesman Jerome.

Arms full of shoe polish, pots, pans, and tea,
he followed Miss Bloom to Room Number 3.

Now THREE rooms of SIX had guests for the night.
To fill up the inn would be pure delight!

$\dfrac{3}{6}$

Knock-knock! went the door. *Ding-dong!* the bell rang.
"Welcome, welcome," Miss Bloom sang.

"In town for my show!" said Trainer P. Klein.
From smallest to LARGEST, his dogs stood in line.

Then Trainer P. Klein and doggies galore
danced down the hall to Room Number 4.

Now FOUR rooms of SIX had guests for the night.
To fill up the inn would be pure delight!

$\dfrac{4}{6}$

Knock-knock! went the door. *Ding-dong!* the bell rang.
"Welcome, welcome," Miss Bloom sang.

"My biggest race ever!" said Johnny Z. Power.
"I hit two-hundred-ten miles per hour!"

Carrying his trophy and pleased to arrive,
he followed Miss Bloom to Room Number 5.

Five rooms of six had guests for the night,
filling Miss Bloom with pure delight.

Then into the kitchen Miss Bloom went to make
a scrumptious dinner for all to partake.

There were chicken and peas, potatoes au gratin,
but the very best part—
Miss Bloom had forgotten!

A strawberry cake
  with whipped cream piled high
still sat on the counter
  when the last dish was dry.

Tired and happy, they all went to bed—
Miss Bloom in Room 6.
"It's a FULL HOUSE," she said.

$$\frac{6}{6} = 1$$

The guests and Miss Bloom all called out,

"Good night!"

plumped up
each pillow,

and
turned off
each light.

But then, in the dark, came shuffles and wiggles,
whispers and mumbles, scuffles and giggles.

Shadows were tiptoeing down the long hall.
But where were they going, bathrobes and all?

Suddenly, Miss Bloom sat up in bed.
"Something's not right at my inn," she said.

She rushed to the kitchen and turned on the light.
There she saw an astonishing sight:

Five out of six–

and the dogs and the cat–

stood covered in cake from toe to top hat.

"Well!" said Miss Bloom, and "Tiddle-ee-dee!

Thank you for saving the last piece

FOR ME!"

$\frac{1}{6}$ $\frac{1}{6}$ $\frac{1}{6}$ $\frac{1}{6}$ $\frac{1}{6}$ $\frac{1}{6}$

$$\frac{6}{6} = 1$$

Dayle Ann Dodds is a former elementary school teacher and holds a degree in early childhood development. She is the author of numerous picture books for children, including *Teacher's Pets; The Great Divide: A Mathematical Marathon;* and *Minnie's Diner: A Multiplying Menu.* About *Full House,* she says, "Fractions were always a little bit difficult for me to understand, so it was fun to write a book to help kids see that a fraction is part of a whole, whether it's one room at an inn or one piece of delicious strawberry cake." Dayle Ann Dodds lives in California.

Abby Carter has illustrated many picture books and chapter books for children, including *My Hippie Grandmother* and the Andy Shane series. She says she was "the kid who was always doodling pictures while taking notes in school," so she never thought she would be illustrating a book about fractions. Abby Carter lives in Connecticut with her husband and two children.